WRESTLE FEST

ILLUSTRATED BY

MICAH PLAYER

 ROARING BROOK PRESS / New York

Ladies and Gentleman,
it's Friday night!

Dinner was pizza.

Annnnd best of all . . .

it's time for . . .

In this corner it's—
DANGEROUS DADDOO!

He's mad. He's bad.
He's *DAD.*

Over on the kid crew we have—THE TAG TEAM TWINS. Featuring the nutty-by-nature PEANUT BROTHER and the wriggly-giggly JELLYFISH

with special guest star . . . BIG BALD BABY!

Kicking things off tonight is Jellyfish. She lands a **JUMPIN' JELLYFLOP** on her poor old pop!

Yessirree, Dangerous Daddoo is smack dab in a
WHAM BAM JAM SLAM-WICH!

PEANUT, PEANUT BROTHER...

AND JELLY!

The tides—and tentacles—quickly turn!

Peanut Brother spins
in to help his sis with a
SWIRLING
SHARK-CLONE.

TOTALLY
JAWSOME!

BUT HOLD THE TARTAR SAUCE!

What's going on . . . ?

From out of nowhere it's a

FLYING MOM BOMB!

That's right folks, the one, the only MAMA-RAMAAAAAA has entered the ring! She's home from work and going berserk.

Are TWO grown-ups TOO many for the Tag Team Twins?
Does this mean beddy—BYE-BYE for the kid crew?

Dangerous Daddoo looks like he's got this one in the bag.

But hold the **BANANA-PHONE!** Could it be?

Dangerous Daddoo's been DOUBLE-CROSSED.

It's a perfect

PARENT
TRAP!

Bedtime looks bleak.

Daddoo is da-DONE.

Ladies and gentlemen, nothing can save him now.

Nothing except Big Bald Baby and a . . .

After a quick
BEDTIME BLITZ –

JAMMIE JAM

BRUSH-*n*-FLUSH

BOOK-n-TUCK

—this wrestlefest has officially become a *nestle*fest.

It's Friday night lights out for the kid crew.

Goodnight from the arena, until next week's . . .

FRIDAY NIGHT

(Goodnight)

Text copyright © 2020 by J. F. Fox
illustrations copyright © 2020 by Micah Player
Published by Roaring Brook Press
Roaring Brook Press is a division of Holtzbrinck Publishing
Holdings Limited Partnership
120 Broadway, New York, NY 10271
mackids.com

Library of Congress Control Number: 2019941016

ISBN: 978-1-250-21240-5

Our books may be purchased in bulk for promotional, educational, or
business use. Please contact your local bookseller or the Macmillan
Corporate and Premium Sales Department at (800) 221-7945 ext. 5442
or by e-mail at MacmillanSpecialMarkets@macmillan.com.

First edition, 2020
Book design by Monique Sterling
Printed in China by RR Donnelley Asia Printing Solutions Ltd.,
Dongguan City, Guangdong Province

1 3 5 7 9 10 8 6 4 2